sermons of great people

Abdul Waheed

Sermons of Great people

Abdul Waheed

CERTIFICATE OF PUBLISHING

We're proud to present this certificate of publishing to

Abdul Waheed

for successfully publishing

SERMONS OF GREAT PEOPLE

on. 20-01-2023

"A writer's life and work are not a gift to mankind; **they're a necessity**" ~ Toni Morrison

Dedication

This book is dedicated to the memory of my late father Haji Ubairdur Rahman (Munna) and younger brother Abdul Hameed. May God (Allah) give peace to his soul.

Aamen

Table of contents

Preface

Every religion of the world has some or the other avatar or prophet or messenger who guides people by giving holy teachings and this is the core of that religion. If a man does not follow the teachings, then he is rejected from the religion.

 Please read this book on this subject and make use of it. Inform immediately if any defect is found.

Thanks -

Date - 21/12/2022

Preaching of Hazrat Muhammad Sahib (Islam Religion)

Regrettably, many people claim to be Muslims, but very few follow the teachings of Islam. The one who read the prayers five times started considering himself as a staunch Muslim.

But look at the condition laid down by the Qur'an to be a Muslim -- it is in Surah Baqarah -- "Righteousness and goodness is not only in praying facing east or west. Rather, the real righteousness and virtue is that:

1- Believe in Allah (God).

2- On the last day i.e. on this the good deeds of the honest will be rewarded and the bad deeds will be punished.

3--Believe in the angels (because it was through them that God's speech reached the prophets).

4- Believe in the book of Allah (Quran Pak).

5- Have faith in all the messengers sent by Allah.

6-- As a proof of love for Allah, help your relatives, orphans, destitute people, travelers and beggars with goods and money and free the slaves - then also keep offering prayers, Zakat (religious tax which is given only to the poor) Keep doing Shraddha, when you make a promise to someone, then fulfill it. Work with patience in times of poverty, suffering and trouble. The one who follows these things will be a true Muslim and will be called a virtuous person.

Here are some examples of what Islam has said to cure these ills of the society.
1 -- God dislikes it very much that you say do something, don't say such things which you cannot do.
2 -Don't present the lie with the truth.

3 - If you know the truth then don't try to hide it.

4 - God's curse on the one who tells a lie.

5 -- Truth is the basis of faith.

6 -- Telling lies and getting people to fight are the actions of low level of humanity.

7 -- Don't make fun of each other, who knows if the person you are making fun of is better than you.

8- A woman should not laugh at another woman because the one you laugh at may be better than you.

9- Do not keep track of each other.

10- Do not speak ill of each other behind the back because it is like eating the flesh of one's dead brother.

11- Do not misbehave on anyone (do not think bad without investigation because it is a big sin).

12- Accusing the innocent is a great sin.

13 - The one who conducts well is near to God and is liked by Him.

14 -- The one who increases love and goodwill among himself is near to God and the one who does evil behind the back and makes friends fight with each other will never go to heaven. Imam Muhammad Bakr has said that "he who does evil behind his back is forbidden heaven" Hazrat Ali has said "the tongue is the scales of a man, keep it balanced"In Quran, good and evil can never be equal.

Received well even from the one who did evil. In this way, the enmity between you and the enemy can turn into love. In brief, Kuryan has condemned cheating, tyranny, fight, riot, misconduct, theft, gambling and alcohol in Amanat and has emphasized on love, harmony, forgiveness and equality and peace, through this a healthy society and good environment can be created. . Islam has said that non-Muslims should also be treated well. In Surah Kahf, Allah has said that "O Prophet of the infidels, Allah is well aware of what is said about you. Still, don't put any pressure on them. Recite the Qur'an only to those people who keep in their hearts the fear of the day on which Allah will settle accounts.

Enmity can turn into love. In short, Kuryan has condemned cheating, tyranny, fight, riot, misconduct, theft, gambling and alcohol in trust and has emphasized on love, harmony, forgiveness and equality and peace, through this a healthy society and good environment can be created. . Islam has told that non-Muslims should also be treated well. In Surah Kahf, Allah has said that "O Prophet of the infidels, Allah is well aware of what they say about you. Still, do not put any pressure on them. Only those people keep reciting the Qur'an who have the fear of that Day in their hearts." Let's keep the day when Allah will settle the accounts.

2-- O Muslims, those who remember gods other than God -- do not say bad things to them, otherwise they will retaliate or say bad things to your God out of ignorance. 3- O Muslims, do not fight with the Holy Book (on which God has revealed the book for guidance) – but find a solution to the problem in a good way among yourselves.

,

4- If the Mushreekin (who worship many gods along with God) seek refuge from you, give them refuge. Tell him the words of Allah, explain and then take him to a place of peace. When Hazrat Ali was Caliph. At that time he sent instructions to the governor of Egypt.

 Five remedies for abstinence and self-control: In these verses (verses of the Holy Quran), God not only guides us through excellent teachings to reach the path of righteousness, but also tells us five remedies to make us self-controlled and of good character. Protect your eyes from looking at other women. 2. To save the Shrutputs from listening to the voices of other's nameless women.

3. Don't listen to the stories of nameless strangers.

 4. Avoiding all such meetings and gatherings in which this misdeed is likely to happen.

5. If there is no marriage, keep a fast etc.

At this juncture we say this with absolute certainty that this beautiful teaching with all the means which the Holy Qur'an has described is exclusive to Islam alone.

Tafsir of holy Quran

Tafsir ibne kathir

Sura Aal e imran 3, ayat 110

Virtues of the Ummah of Muhammad صلى الله عليه وسلم, the Best Nation Ever

Allah states that the Ummah of Muhammad is the best nation ever,

كُنتُمْ خَيْرَ أُمَّةٍ أُخْرِجَتْ لِلنَّاسِ

You are the best of peoples ever raised up for mankind,

Al-Bukhari recorded that Abu Hurayrah commented on this Ayah,

"(You, Muslims, are) the best nation of people for the people, you bring them tied in chains on their necks (capture them in war) and they later embrace Islam."

Similar was said by Ibn Abbas, Mujahid, Atiyah Al-Awfi, Ikrimah, Ata and Ar-Rabi bin Anas that,

كُنتُمْ خَيْرَ أُمَّةٍ أُخْرِجَتْ لِلنَّاسِ

(You are the best of peoples ever raised up for mankind),

means, the best of peoples for the people.

The meaning of the Ayah is that the Ummah of Muhammad is the most righteous and beneficial nation for mankind. Hence Allah's description of them,

تَأْمُرُونَ بِالْمَعْرُوفِ وَتَنْهَوْنَ عَنِ الْمُنكَرِ وَتُؤْمِنُونَ بِاللَّهِ

you enjoin Al-Ma'ruf and forbid Al-Munkar and believe in Allah.

Ahmad, At-Tirmidhi, Ibn Majah, and Al-Hakim recorded that Hakim bin Muawiyah bin Haydah narrated that his father said that the Messenger of Allah said,

أَنْتُمْ تُوَفُّونَ سَبْعِينَ أُمَّةً أَنْتُمْ خَيْرُهَا وَأَنْتُمْ أَكْرَمُ عَلَى اللهِ عَزَّ وَجَل

You are the final of seventy nations, you are the best and most honored among them to Allah.

This is a well-known Hadith about which At-Tirmidhi said, "Hasan", and which is also narrated from Mu'adh bin Jabal and Abu Sa'id.

The Ummah of Muhammad achieved this virtue because of its Prophet, Muhammad, peace be upon him, the most regarded of Allah's creation and the most honored Messenger with Allah. Allah sent Muhammad with the perfect and complete Law that was never given to any Prophet or Messenger before him. In Muhammad's Law, few deeds take the place of the many deeds that other nations performed. For instance, Imam Ahmad recorded that Ali bin Abi Talib said,

"The Messenger of Allah said,

أُعْطِيتُ مَا لَمْ يُعْطَ أَحَدٌ مِنَ الْأَنْبِيَاء

I was given what no other Prophet before me was given.

We said, 'O Messenger of Allah! What is it?'

He said,

نُصِرْتُ بِالرُّعْبِ

وَأُعْطِيتُ مَفَاتِيحَ الْأَرْضِ

وَسُمِّيتُ أَحْمَدَ

وَجُعِلَ التُّرَابُ لِي طَهُورًا

وَجُعِلَتْ أُمَّتِي خَيْرَ الأُمَم

I was given victory by fear,

I was given the keys of the earth,

I was called Ahmad,

the earth was made a clean place for me (to pray and perform Tayammum with it),

and my Ummah was made the best Ummah."

The chain of narration for this Hadith is Hasan.

There are several Hadiths that we should mention here.

The Two Sahihs recorded that Az-Zuhri said that, Sa'id bin Al-Musayyib said that Abu Hurayrah narrated to him,

"I heard the Messenger of Allah saying,

يَدْخُلُ الْجَنَّـةَ مِنْ أُمَّتِي زُمْرَةٌ وَهُمْ سَبْعُونَ أَلْفًا تُضِيءُ وُجُوهُهُمْ إِضَاءَةَ الْقَمَرِ لَيْلَةَ الْبَدْرِ

A group of seventy thousand from my Ummah will enter Paradise, while their faces are radiating, just like the moon when it is full.'

Ukkashah bin Mihsan Al-Asadi stood up, saying, 'O Messenger of Allah! Supplicate to Allah that I am one of them.'

The Messenger of Allah said,

اللَّهُمَّ اجْعَلْهُ مِنْهُم

'O Allah! Make him one of them.'

A man from the Ansar also stood and said, 'O Messenger of Allah! Supplicate to Allah that I am one of them.'

The Messenger said,

سَبَقَكَ بِهَا عُكَّاشَة

Ukkashah has beaten you to it.'

Another Hadith that Establishes the Virtues of the Ummah of Muhammad in this Life and the Hereafter

Imam Ahmad recorded that Jabir said,

"I heard the Messenger of Allah saying,

إِنِّي لَأَرْجُو أَنْ يَكُونَ مَنْ يَتَّبِعُنِي مِنْ أُمَّتِي يَوْمَ الْقِيَامَةِ رُبُعَ الْجَنَّـةِ

'I hope that those who follow me will be one-fourth of the residents of Paradise on the Day of Resurrection.'

We said, 'Allahu Akbar'.

He then said,

أَرْجُو أَنْ يَكُونُوا ثُلُثَ النَّاس

'I hope that they will be one-third of the people.'

We said, 'Allahu Akbar'.

He then said,

أَرْجُو أَنْ تَكُونُوا الشَّطْر

'I hope that you will be one-half.'"

Imam Ahmad recorded the same Hadith with another chain of narration, and this Hadith meets the criteria of Muslim in his Sahih.

In the Two Sahihs, it is recorded that Abdullah bin Mas`ud said,

"The Messenger of Allah said to us,

أَمَا تَرْضَوْنَ أَنْ تَكُونُوا رُبُعَ أَهْلِ الْجَنَّةِ

Does it please you that you will be one-fourth of the people of Paradise?

We said, `Allahu Akbar!'

He added,

أَمَا تَرْضَوْنَ أَنْ تَكُونُوا ثُلُثَ أَهْلِ الْجَنَّةِ

Does it please you that you will be one-third of the people of Paradise?

We said, 'Allahu Akbar!'

He said,

إِنِّي لَأَرْجُو أَنْ تَكُونُوا شَطْرَ أَهْلِ الْجَنَّةِ

I hope that you will be half of the people of Paradise."

Another Hadith

Imam Ahmad recorded that Buraydah said that;

the Prophet said,

أَهْلُ الْجَنَّةِ عِشْرُونَ وَمِائَةُ صَفَّ هذِهِ الْأُمَّةُ مِنْ ذلِكَ ثَمَانُونَ صَفًّا

The people of Paradise are one hundred and twenty rows, this Ummah takes up eighty of them.

Imam Ahmad also collected this Hadith through another chain of narration.

At-Tirmidhi and Ibn Majah also collected this Hadith, and At-Tirmidhi said, this Hadith is Hasan.

Abdur-Razzaq recorded that Abu Hurayrah said that,

the Prophet said,

نَحْنُ الآخِرُونَ الأَوَّلُونَ يَوْمَ الْقِيَامَةِ نَحْنُ أَوَّلُ النَّاسِ دُخُولاً الْجَنَّـةَ بَيْدَ أَنَّهُمْ أُوتُوا الْكِتَابَ مِنْ قَبْلِنَا وَأُوتِينَاهُ مِنْ بَعْدِهِمْ فَهَدَانَا اللهُ لِمَا اخْتَلَفُوا فِيهِ مِنَ الْحَقِّ

فَهَذَا الْيَوْمُ الَّذِي اخْتَلَفُوا فِيهِ النَّاسُ لَنَا فِيهِ تَبَعٌ غَدًا لِلْيَهُودِ وَلِلنَّصَارَى بَعْدَ غَدٍ

We (Muslims) are the last to come, but the foremost on the Day of Resurrection, and the first people to enter Paradise, although the former nations were given the Scriptures before us and we after them. Allah gave us the guidance of truth that they have been disputing about.

This (Friday) is the Day that they have been disputing about, and all the other people are behind us in this matter:the Jews' (day of congregation is) tomorrow (Saturday) and the Christians' is the day after tomorrow (Sunday).

Al-Bukhari and Muslim collected this Hadith.

Muslim recorded Abu Hurayrah saying that the Messenger of Allah said,

نَحْنُ الْأَخِرُونَ الْأَوَّلُونَ يَوْمَ الْقِيَامَةِ نَحْنُ أَوَّلُ مَنْ يَدْخُلُ الْجَنَّـةَ

We (Muslims) are the last (to come), but (will be) the foremost on the Day of Resurrection, and will be the first people to enter Paradise... until the end of the Hadith.

These and other Hadiths conform to the meaning of the Ayah,

كُنتُمْ خَيْرَ أُمَّةٍ أُخْرِجَتْ لِلنَّاسِ تَأْمُرُونَ بِالْمَعْرُوفِ وَتَنْهَوْنَ عَنِ الْمُنكَرِ وَتُؤْمِنُونَ بِاللَّهِ

(You are the best of peoples ever raised up for mankind; you enjoin Al-Ma`ruf (all that Islam has ordained) and forbid Al-Munkar (all that Islam has forbidden), and you believe in Allah).

Therefore, whoever among this Ummah acquires these qualities, will have a share in this praise.

Qatadah said,

"We were told that Umar bin Al-Khattab recited this Ayah (3:110) during a Hajj that he performed, when he saw that the people were rushing. He then said, 'Whoever likes to be among this (praised) Ummah, let him fulfill the condition that Allah set in this Ayah.'"

Ibn Jarir recorded this.

Those from this Ummah who do not acquire these qualities will be just like the People of the Scriptures whom Allah criticized, when He said,

كَانُواْ لَا يَتَنَاهَوْنَ عَن مُّنكَرٍ فَعَلُوهُ

(They did not forbid one another from the Munkar which they committed... (5:79).

This is the reason why, after Allah praised the Muslim Ummah with the qualities that He mentioned, He criticized the People of the Scriptures and chastised them, saying,

وَلَوْ امَنَ أَهْلُ الْكِتَابِ

And had the People of the Scripture (Jews and Christians) believed,

in what was sent down to Muhammad.

لَكَانَ خَيْرًا لَّهُم مِّنْهُمُ الْمُوْمِنُونَ وَأَكْثَرُهُمُ الْفَاسِقُونَ

it would have been better for them; among them are some who have faith, but most of them are Fasiqun (rebellious).

Therefore only a few of them believe in Allah and in what was sent down to you and to them. The majority of them follow deviation, disbelief, sin and rebellion.

The Good News that Muslims will Dominate the People of the Book

While delivering the good news to His believing servants that victory and dominance will be theirs against the disbelieving, atheistic People of the Scriptures, Allah then said,

لَن يَضُرُّوكُمْ إِلاَّ أَذًى وَإِن يُقَاتِلُوكُمْ يُوَلُّوكُمُ الأَدْبَارَ ثُمَّ لَا يُنصَرُونَ

Tafsir Abu Bakr Al-Jazairi3
Surah Al Imran 3, ayat 110

Abu Bakr Al-Jazairi (b. 1921 AD)
Abu Bakr al-Jaza'iri (d. 2018 AD), a first-stage compiler and reviewer.

words explanation:

You were the best nation: you were the best and most blessed nation that ever existed on earth.

It was brought out to the people: it was revealed and highlighted to guide and benefit people.

Harm: minor harm.
They turn their backs to you: they are defeated and flee from the battle, and they turn their backs to you.

Humiliation struck them: Humiliation surrounded them and stuck to them so that it would not leave them.

They were plagued with anger: They returned from their long journey of disbelief and doing evil with the wrath of God.

That is because they...etc.: This is a reference to the humiliation and poverty that befell them and the wrath of God Almighty that they were subjected to and the torment that followed. (The ba) means that they are caused by it, that is, because of their doing such and such, and poverty is the humiliation of want and poverty.

They transgress: transgression exceeds the limit in injustice, evil, and corruption.

Meaning of the verses:

When God Almighty commanded the believers to fear Him and adhere to His rope, so they complied, and He commanded them to form a group of them who would call to Islam and enjoin what is right and forbid what is wrong, so they complied. He reminded them of great goodness, and He said to them: {You were the best of a nation brought forth for mankind} just as the Messenger of God, may God bless him and grant him peace, said to them: "You were the best of people for mankind." .. "And he described them as the best nation in which they were, and said: You command what is right, which is Islam, and the laws of guidance that His Prophet, may God bless him and grant him peace, brought, and you forbid what is wrong, which is disbelief, polytheism, and major sins and immoralities, and you believe in God. And what belief in God entails is belief in everything that God Almighty has commanded belief in, such as angels, books, messengers, the afterlife, and destiny. Then God Almighty called the People of the Book to the true faith that saves them from the punishment of God, and He Almighty said: If the People of the Book believed in the Prophet Muhammad and the Islam he brought, it would be better for them than the false claim of faith that they claim. And God Almighty told him that among them are believers who are sincere in their faith, such as Abdullah bin Salam and his brother, and Tha'labah bin Saeed and his brother, and most of them are immoral people who did not act according to what was stated in their Book of doctrines and laws, including that God Almighty commanded to believe in the illiterate Prophet and followed.

sermon is a religious discourse or oration by a preacher, usually a member of clergy. Sermons address a scriptural, theological, or moral topic, usually expounding on a type of belief, law, or behavior within both past and present contexts. Elements of the sermon often include exposition, exhortation, and practical application. The act of delivering a sermon is called preaching. In secular usage, the word sermon may refer, often disparagingly, to a lecture on morals.

A Roadside Sermon by John Pettie
In Christian practice, a sermon is usually preached to a congregation in a place of worship, either from an elevated architectural feature, known as a pulpit or an ambo, or from behind a lectern. The word sermon comes from a Middle English word which was derived from Old French, which in turn originates from the Latin word sermō meaning 'discourse.' A sermonette is a short sermon (usually associated with television broadcasting, as stations would present a sermonette before signing off for the night). The Christian Bible contains many speeches without interlocution, which some take to be sermons: Jesus' Sermon on the Mount in Matthew 5–7 (though the gospel writers do not specifically call it a sermon; the popular descriptor for Jesus' speech there came much later); and Peter after Pentecost in Acts 2:14–40 (though this speech was delivered to

non-Christians and as such is not quite parallel to the popular definition of a sermon).

In Islam, sermons are known as khutbah.

Types of sermons

There are a number of different types of sermons, that differ both in their subject matter and by their intended audience, and accordingly not every preacher is equally well-versed in every type. The types of sermons are:

Biographical sermons – tracing the story of a particular biblical character through a number of parts of the Bible.

Evangelistic sermons (associated with the Greek word kerygma) – seeking to convert the hearers or bring them back to their previous faith through a recounting of the foundational story of the religion, in Christianity, the Good News.

Expository preaching – exegesis, that is sermons that expound and explain a text to the congregation.

Historical sermons – which seek to portray a biblical story within its non-biblical historical perspective.

Hortatory sermons (associated with the Greek word didache) – exhort a return to living ethically, in Christianity a return to living on the basis of the gospel.

Illuminative sermons, also known as proems (petihta) – which connect an apparently unrelated biblical verse or religious question with the current calendrical event or festival.

Liturgical sermons – sermons that explain the liturgy, why certain things are done during a service, such as why communion is offered and what it means.

Narrative sermons – which tell a story, often a parable, or a series of stories, to make a moral point.

Redemptive-historical preaching – sermons that take into consideration the context of any given text within the broader history of salvation as recorded in the canon of the bible.

Topical sermons – concerned with a particular subject of current concern;

Sermons can be both written and spoken out loud.

Khutbah serves as the primary formal occasion for public preaching in the Islamic tradition. In societies or communities with (for example) low literacy rates, strong habits of communal worship, and/or limited mass-media, the preaching of sermons throughout networks of congregations can have important informative and prescriptive propaganda functions for both civil and religious authorities—which may regulate the manner, frequency, licensing, personnel and content of preaching accordingly.

Dat erste Capittel.

Yth ys de Apenbarynge Jhesu Christi / de eme Godt gegeuen hefft / synen knechten kunt tho dönde / wat in kort schal / vnde hefft se betekent vnde gesent dorch synen Engel tho synem knechte Johannes / de betüget hefft dat wort Gades / vnde dat tüchenisse van Jhesu Christo / wat he gesen hefft / Salich ys de dar lyst vn̄ de dar hören de wort der wissegynge / vnde beholden wat darynne gescreuen ys / wente de tydt ys harde by.

Johannes / den söuen vorsammelingen in Asia / Gnade sy mit juw vnde frede / van dem de dar ys / vnde de dar was / vnde de dar kumpt / vnde van den söuen geysten / de dar synt vor synem stole / vnde van Jhesu Christo / de dar ys de truwe tüge vnde erstgeboerne van den doden / vnde eyn vörste aller könynge vp erden / de vns geleuet hefft vnde gewasschen van den sünden / mit synem blode / vnde hefft vns tho könyngen

Isa Masih (Jesus Christ), Christianity

Jesus began his Sermon on the Mount with the following Beatitudes, or Christian perfection or holiness, which serve as guiding pillars for every Christian:- (1) Blessed are those who are poor, because the kingdom of heaven belongs to them.

(2) Blessed are those who mourn, for they will be comforted.

(3) Blessed are those who are humble, for they will become the possessors of the earth.

(4) Blessed are those who hunger and thirst for righteousness, for they will be satisfied.

(5) Blessed are those who are merciful, for they will receive mercy.

(6) Blessed are those whose hearts are pure, for they shall see the Supreme Lord.

(7) Blessed are those who make peace, because they will be called the sons of God.

(8) Blessed are those who are punished for righteous conduct, for theirs is the kingdom of heaven. Here Jesus tells us that those who bring peace or reconciliation should not become peace breakers or divisive. Because peace is a condition in which people are not allowed any kind of violence that disturbs their steady concern. Peace can be personal (spiritual) or it can be social. Social peace is a reciprocal contract with one another by which we refrain from harming one another (6:34). It is also freedom from strife, and rest from oppression (12:14), spiritual peace from sin, which Through our enmity with God, there is salvation (5:1) which results in peace of mind. (10:22) | This peace is a gift of God received through Jesus Christ. (2, 3, 16) In religious texts, the word Shanti is generally used in the sense of public or personal quietness and unperturbedness, but often prosperity and happiness of every kind and every degree are also called peace as we do. That "May you rest in peace, rest in peace."

American civil rights activist **Martin Luther King** Jr. is also called the Gandhi of America. He fought a long battle against racism. He was awarded the Nobel Prize at the age of just 35 for leading a non-violent movement against apartheid and racism prevalent in American society. Martin Luther King is the first person to receive the Nobel Prize at the youngest age. He donated the money received under the Nobel Prize to civil rights movements. The thoughts of Martin Luther King Jr. can fill life with positive energy. His thoughts inspire to fight all difficulties.

1-If you can't fly, then run. If you can't run, then walk. If you can't walk, then crawl. But always keep moving forward.

2. We must learn to live together as brothers or we will all perish as fools.

3- Love is the only force that can turn an enemy into a friend.

4. Darkness can never drive out darkness. Only light can drive out darkness. Similarly, hate cannot drive out hate. Only love can drive out hate.

In Christianity,

a sermon is typically identified as an address or discourse delivered to a congregation of Christians, typically containing theological or moral instruction. The sermon by Christian orators was partly based on the tradition of public lectures by classical orators. Although it is often called a homily, the original distinction between a sermon and a homily was that a sermon was delivered by a clergyman (licensed preacher) while a homily was read from a printed copy by a layman. In the 20th century the distinction has become one of the sermon being likely to be longer, have more structure, and contain more theological content. Homilies are usually considered to be a type of sermon, usually narrative or biographical

The word sermon is used contemporarily to describe many famous moments in Christian (and Jewish) history. The most famous example is the Sermon on the Mount by Jesus of Nazareth. This address was given around 30 AD, and is recounted in the Gospel of Matthew (5:1–7:29, including introductory and concluding material) as being delivered on a mount on the north end of the Sea of Galilee, near Capernaum. It is also contained in some of the other gospel narratives.

During the later history of Christianity, several figures became known for their addresses that later became regarded as sermons.

Examples in the early church include Peter (see especially Acts 2:14b–36), Stephen (see Acts 7:1b–53), Tertullian and John Chrysostom. These addresses were used to spread Christianity across Europe and Asia Minor, and as such are not sermons in the modern sense, but evangelistic messages.

The sermon has been an important part of Christian services since early Christianity, and remains prominent in both Roman Catholicism and Protestantism. Lay preachers sometimes figure in these traditions of worship, for example the Methodist local preachers, but in general preaching has usually been a function of the clergy. The Dominican Order is officially known as the Order of Preachers (Ordo Praedicatorum in Latin); friars of this order were trained to publicly preach in vernacular languages, and the order was created by Saint Dominic to preach to the Cathars of southern France in the early 13th century. The Franciscans are another important preaching order; Travelling preachers, usually friars, were an important feature of late medieval Catholicism. In 1448 the church authorities seated at Angers prohibited open-air preaching in France. If a sermon is delivered during the Mass it comes after the Gospel is sung or read. If it is delivered by the priest or bishop that offers the Mass then he removes his maniple, and in some cases his chasuble, because the sermon is not part of the Mass. A bishop preaches his sermon wearing his mitre while seated whereas a priest, or on rare occasions a deacon, preaches standing and wearing his biretta.In most denominations, modern preaching is kept below forty minutes, but historic preachers of all denominations could at times speak for several hours, and use techniques of rhetoric and theatre that are today somewhat out of fashion in mainline churches.

During the Middle Ages, sermons inspired the beginnings of new religious institutes (e.g., Saint Dominic and Francis of Assisi). Pope Urban II began the First Crusade in November 1095 at the Council of Clermont, France, when he exhorted French knights to retake the Holy Land.

The academic study of sermons, the analysis and classification of their preparation, composition and delivery, is called homiletics.

A controversial issue that aroused strong feelings in early modern Britain was whether sermons should be read from a fully prepared text, or extemporized, perhaps from some notes. Many sermons have been written down, collected and published; published sermons were a major and profitable literary form, and category of books in the book trade, from at least the Late Antique Church to about the late 19th century. Many clergymen openly recycled large chunks of published sermons in their own preaching. Such sermons include John Wesley's Forty-four Sermons, John Chrysostom's Homily on the Resurrection (preached every Easter in Orthodox churches) and Gregory Nazianzus' homily "On the Theophany, or Birthday of Christ" (preached every Christmas in Orthodox churches). The 80 sermons in German of the Dominican Johannes Tauler (1300–1361) were read for centuries after his death.Martin Luther published his sermons (Hauspostille) on the Sunday lessons for the edification of readers. This tradition was continued by Martin Chemnitz and Johann Arndt, as well as many others into the following centuries—for example CH Spurgeon's stenographed sermons, The Metropolitan Tabernacle Pulpit. The widow of Archbishop of Canterbury John Tillotson (1630–1694) received £2,500 for the manuscripts of his sermons, a very large sum.

Lutheranism and Reformed ChristianityThe Reformation led to Protestant sermons, many of which defended the schism with the Roman Catholic Church and explained beliefs about the Bible, theology, and devotion. The distinctive doctrines of Protestantism held that salvation was by faith alone, and convincing people to believe the Gospel and place trust in God for their salvation through Jesus Christ was the decisive step in salvation.

In many Protestant churches, the sermon came to replace the Eucharist as the central act of Christian worship (although some Protestants such as Lutherans give equal time to a sermon and the

Eucharist in their Divine Service). While Luther retained the use of the lectionary for selecting texts for preaching, the Swiss Reformers, such as Ulrich Zwingli, Johannes Oecolampadius, and John Calvin, notably returned to the patristic model of preaching through books of the Bible. The goal of Protestant worship, as conditioned by these reforms, was above all to offer glory to God for the gift of grace in Jesus Christ, to rouse the congregation to a deeper faith, and to inspire them to practice works of love for the benefit of the neighbor, rather than carry on with potentially empty rituals.

Evangelical Christianity

In the 18th and 19th centuries during the Great Awakening, major (evangelistic) sermons were made at revivals, which were especially popular in the United States. These sermons were noted for their "fire-and-brimstone" message, typified by Jonathan Edwards' famous "Sinners in the Hands of an Angry God" speech. In these sermons the wrath of God was intended to be made evident. Edwards also preached on Religious Affections, which discussed the divided Christian world.

In Evangelical Christianity, the sermon is often called the "message". It occupies an important place in worship service, half the time, about 45 to 60 minutes. This message can be supported by a powerpoint, images and videos. In some churches, messages are grouped into thematic series. The one who brings the message is usually a pastor trained either in a bible college or independently. Evangelical sermons are broadcast on the radio, on television channels (televangelism), on the Internet, on web portals, on the website of the churches and through social media like YouTube and Facebook.

Roman Catholic

Roman Catholic preaching has evolved over time but generally the subject matter is similar. As the famous St. Alphonsus Ligouri states, "With regard to the subject matter of sermons. Those subjects should be selected which move most powerfully to detest sin and to love God; whence the preacher should often speak of the last things of death, of judgment, of Hell, of Heaven, and of eternity. According to the advice of the Holy Spirit, 'Remember your last end, and you shall never sin.' (Eccl. vii. 40)."

Among the most famous Catholic sermons are St. Francis of Assisi's Sermon to the Birds, St. Alphonsus Liguori's Italian Sermons for all the Sundays in the year, St. Robert Bellarmine's sermons during the counter-reformation period in Sermons from the Latins, the French

The Sermons of the Curé of Ars by St. John Vianney and the Old English sermons of Ælfric of Eynsham.

THE VEDAS

Preaching of hindu religion

The basis of the teachings given in 'Shikshapatri' are the books 'Sutra Bhashya' and 'Bhagavad Gita' written by Ramanujacharya. ,

The teachings given in 'Shikshapatri' are as follows:

1. Gods and ancestors - do not do violence to goat, deer, rabbit and fish, etc. creatures for the yagya. Non-violence is the ultimate religion.

2. Don't take the offering of meat to the deity to whom alcohol-meat is offered or animals are sacrificed.

3. - Thieves, sinners, drug addicts, hypocrites, lustful and cheaters - never associate with these six types of people.

4. Drink pure water (filtered) and take bath only with pure water.

5. Do not wear clothes that show the inner part of the body.

6. Make sure to read the sources and scriptures of Lord Shri Krishna according to your capacity and capability. ,

7. Vishnu, Shiva, Parvati, Ganapati and Surya- treat these five deities with respect and reverence.

8. Serve your dependent, mother, father, teacher and any person suffering from disease as much as possible throughout your life.

9. Women should not even mention other men even out of instinct.

10. Pativrata Sadhvi women should never show their navel, thigh, breast to other men. Do not keep the body bare or semi-naked.

11. Celibates and sages should not consume paan, opium, tobacco, etc.

ज्ञान
चारित्र
दर्शन
तपस्या
सत्य
अचौर्य
ब्रह्मचर्य
अपरिग्रह
णमो अरिहंताणं,   णमो सिद्धाणं,
णमो आयरियाणं,   णमो उवज्झायाणं,
णमो लोए सव्वसाहूणं,

Teachings of Mahavir Swami - Jainism

Jainism emphasized on the following things

1. The world is eternal and all its substances are mortal.

2. Soul is a step to attain salvation and soul is soul. The soul is pure and the body is impure. The soul gets bound in the body because of false vision, indolence and carelessness.

3. The mind is different from the soul.

4. Attachment and attraction towards actions is the root cause of bondage.

The ultimate goal is to get freedom from 5. Karmas.

6. Free soul is the best.

7. Right faith, right knowledge and right conduct - these three jewels are also the means of attaining salvation. ,

8. According to Jainism, the goal of man is the attainment of Kaivalya Pad (salvation). Salvation is to get rid of past accumulated and present deeds. To achieve this, it is necessary to renounce the

world. According to Jain sages, the soul attains liberation only through its own efforts. Jain monks or devotees who believe in non-violence as the ultimate religion drink water after filtering it. The Jains who are completely vegetarian, while getting up, sitting, walking and moving around take special care that there should be no violence to the living being. They take food before evening. Quotations from the teachings of the Jindevs: --

1. You know the truth One who walks on the path of truth attains immortality.

2. Dharma is the best auspicious among the auspicious and it consists of non-violence, restraint and penance (suppression of desires). Even the gods of heaven bow down to the person whose mind is always righteous.

3. All beings in this world get the fruits of their own deeds, no person, be it a woman or a man, can escape from the good and bad consequences of the deeds done by him.

4. Realizing that life is perishable, do not commit sinful acts. Those who are mindlessly immersed in lust and indulge in sensual pleasures are deceiving themselves because of the effect of self-control.

5. The person who considers all the living beings as self and has equality towards them is worthy of worship.

6-The person who sees, knows and understands all the small and big creatures of the world as his soul, he understands the form of this immense all world. To harm others is to harm yourself, you are the one to kill. You are the one who wants, the one you want to torture is yourself 8. The victory of a person who has conquered himself is greater than that of a person who has conquered thousands and thousands of formidable enemies in a courageous battle. Fight with your inner self, what to fight with external enemies? Happy is the person who has conquered himself.

9- Anger, pride (pride), deceit (maya) and greed (or gluttony) are the four evils that contaminate the soul. Conquer anger with peace, pride with humility (vinaya), deceit with innocence and greed (trishna) with contentment. 10- All the creatures of the world wander outside themselves in search of happiness, but true happiness should be sought in the depths of one's own consciousness.

11. Neither the body is worthy of worship, nor the family, nor the caste. Who will respect a person without virtues? The person who does not have any virtue is neither a sramana nor a shravaka.

12. By not having the slightest ill-feeling towards every living being and wishing for the welfare of all, a true seeker who neither longs for life nor death, gets inspiration for his life and actions. ,

Teachings of taoism

The following ideas about God from the Taoist text are notable

1. I will walk with you to the highest peak of light, where we will reach the true source.

2. As the body is covered by clothes, similarly it has covered the whole world.

3. We want to hear it but cannot hear it. Hence it is 'inaudible'. We want to catch it but cannot catch it. That's why it is called 'untouchable'. The second great follower of Tao was Chuang Chow,

ĐỨC THÁI SƯ
TRẦN QUANG KHẢI

Teachings of confucius

According to Confucius, both knowledge and thinking must go hand in hand because thinking without knowledge is dangerous. He also mentioned the following things*

(I) strange things (II) supernatural power (III) ghosts and gods, etc.

In summary, in Confucianism, where religious customs, ethics, teachings related to family and society have been emphasized, Taoism firmly believes in individualism, the supernatural of God, etc. Both these religions influenced the religious beliefs of the Chinese for a long time, but later their teachings disappeared from China and their place was taken by the tendencies of witchcraft, superstitions and polytheism.

Teachings of Hazrat Musa (Moses) - Judaism

Ten Commandments:

God said:

1. I am the Lord your God.

2. Don't consider anyone other than Me-Jehovah as God. Neither you worship any idol nor anyone else.

3. Do not take the name of your God, Jehovah in vain for any selfishness.

4. You work 6 days a week, rest on the seventh day. Consider the day of rest sacred. Do not do any kind of work on that day. Neither your son-daughter, nor your maid-servant, nor your animals-four-footed, nor the foreigner come to your house, do any work-work.

5. Respect your parents.

6. Don't kill anyone.

7. Don't commit adultery

8. You don't steal.

9. Don't give false testimony.

10. You should neither covet anyone's house nor anyone's wife. Do not covet anyone's slave or maid, nor anyone's bull or donkey. ,

An example of this similarity existing in the spiritual teachings of different religions will be seen in the following quotes: -

Hinduism: "It is the true duty to protect the property of others as one's own property.

Judaism" - "Do to your neighbor what you would not want him to do to you. "Zarathushtra Dharma - "Do as you wish for yourself". ,

Buddhism - One should wish for others the same happiness that he himself wishes for.

"Islam (Muhammadian) religion: "None of you should treat your brother the way he himself would not like to be treated. ,

Bahá'í Faith: Blessed is he who prefers his fellow man to himself.

Human hunger

When a man opens his eyes on this earth, then only different thoughts start arising in his mind. As he grows up, his thoughts start getting serious. He starts thinking different things - 'Who am I? How was born? Where was it before this birth? Where will I go after dying? If God created me, then who is God? How it is ? What is the aim of my life? What is the truth ? What is untruth? what is love ? What is duty? What is irresponsibility? ' Not one such, but many questions arise in our mind. We want their answers. This is the hunger of our mind. Religion is the name of the place from where we hope to get the answers to the questions arising in relation to world-hereafter, God, birth-death, truth-false etc. Religion has been trying to answer all such questions. The foundation of all religions is based on these questions.

Meaning of religion

The word 'Islam' is derived from the word 'Salam'. It means 'peace'. Peaceful acceptance of God. self-sacrifice for him. Surrender to God Erasing the ego and accepting the Self. The word 'Dharma' comes in Vedas - for the thing that holds everyone, for the thing that binds everyone in one thread. 'Religion' also has the same meaning. 'Islam' also goes in the same direction. To know the essence, to know the soul, to know the Supreme Soul is 'religion'. The person who attains this knowledge attains everything. There are different ways to get this knowledge. But there is no need to panic with them. Cow may be black, brown, red, white; Everyone's milk is the same - clean, white and pure. Sweet and lovely!

Teachings of buddhism

People who believe in Lord Buddha are called 'Buddhists'. Lord Buddha did not write any book, his teachings were not even collected for 400 years. Later his main teachings were collected in

Tripitaka and Dhammapada. Gradually there were four sects of Buddhism - Dhervad, Mahayana, Tibetan and Jain. All the four sects believe that Nirvana can be attained only through the Four Noble Truths and the Eightfold Path. The four noble truths are four noble truths.

(1) Grief - Birth, Grief in old age, Disease - Illness, Grief on separation from loved ones, Grief on non-fulfillment of desire.

(2) Sorrow - Samudya - The cause of sorrow is craving to be born again, craving to be happy, craving for various desires.

(3) Suffering - Relinquish the craving completely If the craving is gone, then the sorrow is gone.

(4) Sorrow - Nirodhgamini Pratipada To get rid of sorrow, the way to go towards Nirvana - Ashtangik Marg. Ashtangik Marg There are 8 things in Ashtangik Marg. There are eight ways to attain Nirvana:
1. Samyak Gyan - Knowing the Arya Satya properly.

2. Samyak Sankalp – firm determination

3. Samyak Vachan – speaking the truth. Do not torture anyone with your speech.

4. Samyak Karmant – Avoiding violence, treason and bad conduct.

5. Samyak Aajeev - To earn a living with justice and honesty.

6. Proper Exercise - Always do industry for good deeds. ,

7. Samyak Smriti – Avoiding things like greed etc. that give pain to the mind.

8. Samyak Samadhi - Concentration of the mind except attachment and hatred. To bear in mind

The Twenty-two vows or twenty-two pledges are the 22 Buddhist vows administered by B. R. Ambedkar, the revivalist of Buddhism in India, to his followers. On converting to Buddhism, Ambedkar made 22 vows, and asked his 400,000 supporters to do the same. After receiving lay ordination, Ambedkar gave dhamma diksha to his followers. This ceremony organised on 14 October 1956 in Nagpur included 22 vows administered to all new converts after Three Jewels and Five Precepts. On 16 October 1956, Ambedkar performed another mass religious conversion ceremony at Chandrapur.

Inscription of 22 vows at Deekshabhoomi, Nagpur

It is believed by Ambedkarite Buddhists that these vows are the guidelines of the social revolution that motivates human instincts. These vows demonstrate both the social movement aspect of Navayana Buddhism, and demonstrate its core deviation from earlier sects of Buddhism. In India, these vows are taken as an oath by individuals or groups of people when they convert to Buddhism.

left) On 14 October 1956, Ambedkar administering 22 vows after renouncing Hinduism at Deekshabhoomi, Nagpur; (right) Deekshabhoomi monument, located in Nagpur, Maharashtra where B. R. Ambedkar converted to Buddhism in 1956 is the largest hollow stupa in the world.

22 vows administered by Dr Ambedkar

The following are the 22 vows administered by Ambedkar to his followers:

1- I shall have no faith in Brahma, Vishnu and Maheshwara, nor shall I worship them.

2-I shall have no faith in Rama and Krishna, who are believed to be incarnation of God, nor shall I worship them.

3-I shall have no faith in Gauri, Ganapati and other gods and goddesses of Hindus, nor shall I worship them.

4-I do not believe in the incarnation of God.

5-I do not and shall not believe that Lord Buddha was the incarnation of Vishnu. I believe this to be sheer madness and false propaganda.

6-I shall not perform Shraddha nor shall I give pind.

7-I shall not act in a manner violating the principles and teachings of the Buddha.

8-I shall not allow any ceremonies to be performed by Brahmins.

9-I shall believe in the equality of man.

10-I shall endeavour to establish equality.

11-I shall follow the Noble Eightfold Path of the Buddha.

12-I shall follow the ten paramitas prescribed by the Buddha.

13-I shall have compassion and loving-kindness for all living beings and protect them.

14-I shall not steal.

15-I shall not tell lies.

16-I shall not commit carnal sins.

17-I shall not take intoxicants like liquor, drugs, etc.

(The previous five proscriptive vows [#13–17] are from the Five Precepts.)

18-I shall endeavour to follow the Noble Eightfold Path and practice compassion and loving-kindness in everyday life.

19-I renounce Hinduism, which disfavors humanity and impedes the advancement and development of humanity because it is based on inequality, and adopt Buddhism as my religion.

20-I firmly believe the Dhamma of the Buddha is the only true religion.

21-I consider that I have taken a new birth. (Alternately, "I believe that by adopting Buddhism I am having a re-birth.")

22-I solemnly declare and affirm that I shall hereafter lead my life according to the teachings of Buddha's Dhamma.

Teachings of Zarathushtra (Zoroastrian)

His main teaching was that 'Ahuramazda' is God, who has seven forms or ganas. Those forms or ganas are: light, beautiful knowledge, truth, lordship, purity, well-being and welfare. Later on people made these qualities corporeal and tangible. He continued to propound the principle of monotheism. They did not believe in the principle of worshiping many other deities, such as the sun god named 'Mithra' (friend), the fertility god named 'Anahita' and the Taurus god named 'Haum'. They considered 'mrig' or priests' charity-sacrifice and other worship rituals as useless and pompous. There were neither idols nor temples in ancient Iran. Worship was done under the open sky at the high pyramidal places 'Ziggurat'. His worship method was Havan and prayer. Their religious beliefs and methods of worship seem to have been influenced by the Aryans of the Rigvedic period.

Teachings of Bahá'u'lláh - Bahá'í Faith

The basic teachings of Bahá'í Faith are as follows -

1. That man is 'best', who serves the whole world.

2. The foundation of all religions is the same.

3. God is one . Religion is one. All mankind is one.

4. Every man should keep his outlook universal. Don't keep it narrow. Don't be selfish.

5. Everyone should establish universal brotherhood by renouncing superstition and prejudice.

6. Leaving hatred and narrow-mindedness, all human beings, all nations should live together with love. All problems should be solved with love and harmony.

7. Women and men are equal.

8. Education should be compulsory for all.

9. Everyone's full attention should be paid towards the character development of everyone. Drinking and gambling is prohibited.

10. International governance system, judicial system should be one. International contact - language should be one.

11. The economic system should be such that there should not be too much wealth, not too much poverty and the solution of economic problems should be done from a spiritual point of view.

12. Religion is wise and scientific. Through this world peace can be established.

Precepts inscribed on the temple Baha'i worship - These 9 precepts of Baha'i are inscribed on the nine doors of the building
1. The whole earth is one country and humans are only its citizens.

2. In my view, the best, most dear thing is justice. If you are a lover, stay away from injustice.

3. My love is my fort. The person who enters this fort, remains safe.

4. As long as you are a sinner, don't even think of other's sins.

5. Your heart is my abode. Make it holy, so that I can reside in it.

6. I have made death a messenger of happiness for you, then why are you sad about it?

7. Remember me on my earth, so that I may remember you in my heaven.

8- O the rich of the earth! The poor people among you are my heritage. So you protect this heritage of mine.

9. Knowledge of God is the root source of all knowledge. His talent is excellent.

Teachings of Guru Nanak Ji - Sikhism

The person who sees God everywhere inside and outside, how can his life remain without being pure?   The person who always remembers God, while doing every work, he will think that what I do is right, isn't it? The work I do for my livelihood is sacred, isn't it? Pure life Such a person will lead a pure life only. Will serve others. Will speak the truth Will behave truthfully. He will neither cheat anyone nor torture anyone. Neither will kill anyone, nor will he abuse anyone. His heart will be filled with love, harmony, virtue, service, kindness, compassion and truth. Nanak's order is:

(1) chant the name,

(2) do Kirat and

(3) Vandke Chako. Get the hard earned money - share and eat.

Those who do this, only they get the blessings of the Guru, the Supreme Lord.   Katha and Kirtan, Naam-chanting and Naam-remembrance, Veda recitation and scripture recitation have only one goal to purify the heart, remove the filth from the mind and develop truth, love and compassion in life. If this is there then everything is meaningful, otherwise everything is in vain.

Bibliography

1-world famous religion, opinion and sect

2-way of peace

3- flowers of religions

4- Bahá'í dharm kya kahta hai

5- Judaism says

6- Sikh religion says.

My another books

Sr no.	Book
1	World's Major religions, doctrines and sects
2	An introduction to the Holy Qur'an and it's unsolved mysteries
3	How did humans and language originate ?
4	Islam an introduction and sect
5	Sermons of great people
6	Prayer
7	Allah an introduction
8	Is Al khizr still alive today?
9	Story of harut and marut
10	Grief
11	The mysterious story of Al kahf (Ar raqim)
12	Naming of God

<u>All these books are available in Hindi</u> language and other international languages and are also available in e-book for <u>free on Google Play</u> <u>Store</u>.

My personal introduction

My name is Abdul Waheed, my father's name is Late Haji Ubaidur Rahman and mother's name is Jaibunnisa. I have liked scientific ideology since childhood and have a calm nature and attachment to books. Due to which my curiosity interest has been continuously used in new discoveries and information. I got selected in polytechnic while doing BSc, but unfortunately it remained incomplete because father and brother died. Two words of my father, which are very precious for my life,

<u>first - earn honestly, do not take support of lies, secondly, respect food and eat as much as you want.</u> That's why the education remained incomplete due to the responsibility of the house, then later getting married. Still did not lose courage and today the book is

available in front of you in the form of my thoughts. If any information is left incomplete, please let us know.

Thank you .

Contact-

Abdul Waheed, Barabanki, Uttar Pradesh, India

https://www.facebook.com/profile.php?id=100091298026218